My Cats

by Jane Manners

illustrated by
Steve Haskamp

Harcourt

Orlando Boston Dallas Chicago San Diego

Visit *The Learning Site!*

www.harcourtschool.com

This is me.

Those are my cats.

That's my mom. I can hear her calling me.

My cats hear also.
They hear things that
I can not hear.

My dad makes dinner.
It smells so good.

My cats smell also.
They know that other
cats were here.

I can tell when it is getting dark. My cats know also.

Those cats can see when I can not. They have good eyes.

Those cats are
hungry. I am also.

I know when it's time for bed. My cats know also.

We like to sit together.
My cats are good pals.